DUNBAR SCHOOL LIBRARY
11700 DUNBAR ROAD
GLEN ELLEN, CALIFORNIA

W9-BMT-706

3 3495 00169 5132

First American Edition 1991 by Kane/Miller Book Publishers
Brooklyn, New York & La Jolla, California

Originally published in Spanish under the title *Rosaura En
Bicicleta* by Ediciones Ekaré–Banco del Libro, Caracas, Venezuela

Copyright © 1990 Ediciones Ekaré–Banco del Libro

All rights reserved. For information contact:
Kane/Miller Book Publishers. P.O. Box 529, Brooklyn, N.Y. 11231

Library of Congress Cataloging-in-Publication Data

Barbot, Daniel.
   [Rosaura en bicicleta. English]
   A bicycle for Rosaura / Daniel Barbot, illustrated by Morella
Fuenmayor. — 1st American ed.
      p.   cm.
   Summary: A woman has difficulty finding a bicycle for her pet hen
Rosaura.
   ISBN 0-916291-34-0
   [1. Hens—Fiction.   2. Bicycles—Fiction.   I. Fuenmayor,
Morella, ill. II. Title
PZ7.B2335Bi 1991
  [E]—dc20   90-47215
                                            CIP
                                            AC

Printed and bound in Singapore by Tien Wah Press Pte, Ltd.

2 3 4 5 6 7 8 9 10

DUNBAR SCHOOL LIBRARY
11700 DUNBAR ROAD
GLEN ELLEN, CALIFORNIA 95442

6221

A BICYCLE FOR ROSAURA

Daniel Barbot
Illustrated by Morella Fuenmayor

A CRANKY NELL BOOK

KM Kane/Miller Book Publishers

Brooklyn, New York & La Jolla, California

Señora Amelia loved animals. At home she had a dog, a kitten, a talking parrot, a turtle, twin canaries and a handsome hen named Rosaura.

The month before Rosaura's birthday, Señora Amelia asked, "Have you decided what you'd like for your birthday?"

"Why, yes. A bicycle!" said Rosaura.

"But that's impossible!" Señora Amelia exclaimed. "Who's ever heard of a hen riding a bicycle?"

"That's just it," Rosaura replied. "I want to be the first!"

Señora Amelia wanted to please her hen.

"Tomorrow I will try to find a bicycle for Rosaura," she decided.

Early the next morning she took the bus into the city and stopped in all the bicycle shops. In each and every one she got the same response.

"What? A bicycle for a hen?"

Or, "No way. We don't carry any such model."

Or, "Let's take a look in the catalog. Sorry, señora. They don't make bikes for hens."

So Señora Amelia went home sad and disappointed.

"Rosaura is going to be awfully upset if I have to tell her that I couldn't find her a bicycle," she thought.

As the days passed, Señora Amelia began to think that it *was* hopeless.

Then, one afternoon a strange-looking man came into town. He walked up and down the streets singing and calling:

"I mend old clocks and jack-in-the-boxes.
I repair harmonicas and wind-chimes.
I sharpen penknives and sewing scissors.
I make rollerskates for dogs and eyeglasses for cats."

"Maybe that man can help me," thought Señora Amelia. And she called him over right away.

"What can I do for you señora?" asked the man. "Would you like a singing spoon, a lunar calendar, a chocolate rocking chair . . . . ?"

"No, no," interrupted Señora Amelia. "What I need is . . . a bicycle for my hen."

"Umm . . . Hmmm," murmured the man. "That is a difficult order. I'll have to take measurements. I need to know the length of her legs and the span of her wings."

After jotting down numbers and working out complicated formulas, the man was pleased to announce that he could have the bicycle finished in time for Rosaura's birthday.

The days seemed endless.

Finally, one morning there was a knock at her door. Señora Amelia peeked outside . . . and saw the wonderful bicycle for Rosaura!

She wrapped it up in a big box, tied a bright red ribbon around it, and on the day of Rosaura's birthday . . .

Well, Rosaura was delighted with her present. Now, every morning she rides to the grocery store to buy milk and bread for Señora Amelia.

So, if you should ever visit this town in
Venezuela, you're sure to see Rosaura speeding by on
her bicycle. But . . . watch out! The strange man
forgot the brakes!